# The Wild Life.

A line in the sand.

For Leo, with love xx

Omnibus Books
an imprint of Scholastic Australia Pty Ltd
(ABN 11 000 614 577)
PO Box 579, Gosford NSW 2250.
www.scholastic.com.au

Part of the Scholastic Group • Sydney • Auckland • New York • Toronto • London
Mexico City • New Delhi • Hong Kong • Buenos Aires • Puerto Rico

Published by Scholastic Australia in 2022.


NATIONAL LIBRARY OF AUSTRALIA

A catalogue record for this book is available from the National Library of Australia

ISBN: 978-1-76120-962-8

Typeset in New Clarendon and French Fries.

Printed in China by Asia Pacific Offset.
Scholastic Australia's policy, in association with Asia Pacific Offset, is to use papers that are renewable and made efficiently from wood grown in responsibly managed forests, so as to minimise its environmental footprint.

10 9 8 7 6 5 4 24 25 26 / 2

Queensland Government

This project is supported by the Queensland Government through Arts Queensland.

We acknowledge the traditional custodians of the land on which we live and work, and pay respect to the Gubbi Gubbi nation. We pay respects to the Elders of the community and extend our recognition to their descendants.
Laura and Philip Bunting.

Story by Laura Bunting.
Illustrations by Philip Bunting.

# The Wild Life.

## A line in the sand.

An Omnibus book from
Scholastic Australia.

# PART 1

(In which Nature calls)

Wombat was enjoying the most refreshing sleep of his life. In his dreams he was swimming. No, not swimming, he was splishing, sploshing and splashing. He waded through the waves, soaked in the shallows, and frolicked in the foam. He laughed giddily as he let the cool water trickle over his head.

All at once, a strange sensation roused him from his slumber.

Urgency. Down below.

Wombat's tank was full.
His bladder was bursting.
Hey Diddle Diddle, he needed a …

Yes, Nature was calling. But now may not have been the best time to answer the call.

Wombat crossed his legs tightly,
and held on.

Then, he cautiously poked his head out of his burrow.

"Midday! Just as I suspected," he grumbled.

The light was so bright compared to the darkness of his burrow, that his pupils shrivelled in shock.

Fig. 1. A very unscientific cross-section detailing the interior of wombat's eyeballs.

Wombat bumbled around blindly, accidentally reversing outside his burrow and onto the dirt. Dirt so hot, his paws sizzled like sausages the moment they touched it.

"Hot!
Hot!
Hot!"

he cried.

"Ouchy!
Ouchy!
Ouchy!"

he yelped.

"Oowwweeeee!"

he wailed, hopping around in panicked circles, spinning further and further away from the cool shade of his burrow.

Wombat was still unable to see,
but he was very much able to **feel**
the unmistakable sensation of
being barbecued.

Meanwhile, Roo was relaxing under the fast-disappearing shade of a gum tree.

She stretched slowly, scratched her belly and lazily sniffed at the air.

"Wombat? Are you cooking something?"

"Yes!" cried Wombat.

"I'm cooking ... me!

I shouldn't know what Cooked Me smells like! Help!"

"Oh, Wombat," said Roo, smiling and shaking her head as she hopped slowly towards him. "It can't be that hot!"

But as she left her shady spot behind and neared Wombat, her smile disappeared and her eyes widened in panic.

"Hot!
Hot!
Hot!"

she cried.

"Ai! Ai! Ai!"

she yelped.

"Oowweee!"

she wailed, hopping
wildly from paw to paw.

"Wombat! What on earth are you doing out here in the middle of the day?"

"I needed to go ..." shrieked Wombat.

"Go **where?**" cried Roo.

"I needed to ... **go!**" said Wombat as slowly and carefully as he could muster.

"I know! **Where?**" cried Roo.

“Go pee pee!”

shouted Wombat in sheer exasperation.

For a moment, Roo stopped bouncing and scratched her head. “Wait, you mean that enormous burrow of yours doesn’t even have a loo?”

"What? No! Of course not. What kind of animal goes to the toilet where they sleep?!" scoffed Wombat.

Roo blushed.

"It doesn't matter anyway!" cried Wombat. "At this point, I'm less worried about a puddle of pee than a puddle of me!"

"Right, quick!
Back to the shade,"

exclaimed Roo. But as she swung around in panic ...

# Thwack!

Her powerful tail clocked Wombat so hard it sent him flying, like an enormous, hairy cricket ball.

# PART 2

## (In which Wombat crash lands)

*I'm pretty sure I should feel terrified*, thought Wombat as he sailed through the air to his certain death …

but this cool breeze feels
amazing on my paws!

Fortunately for Wombat,
a small, dense pocket
of scrub broke his fall.
He landed with a hard

**thud!**

Which was far better than the

messy splatter

he was predicting.

Wombat dusted himself off, marvelling at the fact that he'd escaped with barely a bruise …

when a huge coconut dropped on his head.

# PART 3

(In which Wombat discovers he is not alone)

A while later, Wombat woke, panicked and sweaty. This wasn't unusual for Wombat, even when he hadn't just been attacked by a coconut.

**Where am I?** he thought,
scratching his head.

"Ow!" he yelped as his paw touched the tender lump.

He tried to remember what had happened, and looked around nervously for the beast who had assaulted him, when he heard strange noises just beyond the bushes …

"Aaaa!
Aaaa!
Eeeee!
Eee!"

"Aaaa! Eeee! Oooo!"

The bushes started shaking.
The thing kept wailing.

Wombat froze, then felt a warm, wet sensation trickle down his leg. An unsettling mix of relief, regret and absolute terror rushed through him.

Then, out of the bushes, the beast emerged ...

and fell flat on its belly.

"Roo!"

cried Wombat.

"Wombat!"

cried Roo, as fat tears welled in her eyes.

"I can't tell if you're happy or sad to see me!" said Wombat.

"So happy!" cried Roo. Then she shuffled onto her bottom and whimpered.

"Oh, Roo!" gasped Wombat. "Your paws! We need to put them in cold water – they're **glowing!**"

"I know," said Roo sadly. "So are yours!

But where are we going to find water around here? I don't even know where we are!"

Wombat suddenly froze again and stared blankly ahead. It looked like he had just died, standing up, with his eyes open.

"Are you okay, Wombat?" asked Roo, waving her paws in front of his unblinking eyes.

"I feel strange," said Wombat. "Like I've seen this place before. But that's impossible."

"Maybe you've got deja vu," suggested Roo.

"What?!" wailed Wombat. "Am I dying? Is this my life flashing before my eyes? I'm too young to die! …

I have more burrows to burrow!

More grass to gobble.

More …"

Wombat wracked his brain for a few more life goals. "Well, I guess that's it."

“Deja vu isn’t a disease!” said Roo. “It’s a feeling – you feel like you’ve seen something before, when you know you haven’t.”

“Phhhhh-eee-ewww!” said Wombat, exhaling loudly.

He continued to stare blankly for a bit, then suddenly cried: "No, I actually saw it. When I was flying. I saw ... **water!**"

Wombat and Roo poked their heads through the bushes. "It must be just through …"

"Sand?" said Wombat.

"Waves!" said Roo.

"It's a …"

# “Beach!”

they cried, along with
an unfamiliar voice they
didn’t recognise.

# PART 4

(In which Wombat and Roo encounter a rabbit or a weasel ... or a rabbit-weasel)

Wombat and Roo gazed curiously at the unusual creature in front of them.

"Oh, it's just a … really round rabbit?" whispered Roo uncertainly.

"Looks more like a chubby weasel to me," said Wombat, crouching slightly for a closer look.

The rabbit-weasel hopped up to them. They wished to squish its adorable big cheeks. They longed to stroke its fluffy little ears. They yearned to gently prod its sweet round belly.

"Aww," cooed Roo.

"Look at da cute widdle wabbit-weasel!"

Suddenly, the rabbit-weasel roared.

"Oi!"

It was so loud and terrifying, Wombat leapt into Roo's arms and started sucking his thumb.

"I'm no rabbit and I'm no weasel," said the creature in a surprisingly deep and menacing voice.

"I'm Quokka."

"These here are my associates …

Numbat,

Galah,

and that loose bag of marbles right there is

Yowza.

Word of advice, don't mess with Yowza …

unless you want a first-hand lesson
in how he got his name."

The little crab snapped his pincers threateningly, his eyeballs goggling around hypnotically with each pinch.

"Oh, and one more thing," added Quokka.

"This is my beach!"

"My beach! My beach!"

parroted Galah.

"No! My beach!" said Quokka crossly.

"My beach! My beach!" repeated Galah.

"Silence!" boomed Quokka in irritation.

"Numbat, Yowza, Galah, escort these trespassers off my property!" he ordered fiercely.

"Yes, Sir," said Numbat, punching his tiny fist into his tiny paw.

Galah started screeching wildly.

While Yowza scuttled around, manically snapping his pincers.

"B-b-but, a beach is n-n-n-nature," said Wombat as bravely as he could.

"And n-n-nature belongs to e-e-everyone."

"Oh yeah?" said Quokka.

Then he let out a high-pitched scream, leapt into the air like an out-of-shape furry ninja and stomped hard on Wombat's foot.

Numbat whacked Wombat in the leg.

"Ouch!" yelped Wombat.

Galah feather-slapped Wombat's face.

"Ew! Ew! Ew! Feathers!" cried Wombat.

And Yowza pinched him right on the …

"Yowzaaaaaaaa!"

shouted Wombat.

"Right, that's it, we're out of here, Roo!"

# PART 5

(In which Quokka draws a line in the sand)

As they fled, Wombat glimpsed Roo's pained face as she tried to hop on her badly burnt feet.

Feet she had burned travelling across miles of scorching dirt, just to find him.

His heart filled with gratitude, love and an even more unusual feeling: **brage**. (This is when bravery and rage unite – it's a dangerous little marriage of feelings.) Wombat stopped suddenly.

"Listen here, you greedy little groundhog!" he yelled. "We all found this beach at the same time. It's not **your** beach, it's **everyone's beach**. That's how beaches work!"

"He's right," said Roo, pulling out an important-looking scroll from her pouch.

"Look, it says so right here in

The Rules of Nature!"

"Don't care!" said Quokka. Then he snatched the scroll, scrunched it up, and ate it. Wombat and Roo gasped.

"I think we should just go," whispered Roo, knowing full well that a creature who ate the rules would never agree to live by them.

"That's the first smart idea I've heard all day," said Quokka, looking directly at Wombat. "I think you should listen to your friend."

"My friend," yelled Wombat, "has burnt her feet and needs to soak them in water. There is an ocean of water in front of us. Just let us share this beach! It's … The Right Thing To Do."

Wombat felt the next word catch in his throat like an unwelcome crumb, but he coughed it up for Roo's sake.

"Please?"

"Oh my, such **lovely** manners, Wombat,"

said Quokka dramatically.

"Well, seeing as you asked sooooo nicely, my answer is ...

No!
Nope.
Nah.
Never.
Not on your nelly.
No way!
No how.
Non.
Nein!

Niet!
Nee.
नहीं
不是!
לא!
-. ---
[Inaudible high-pitched squeal.]
[Passes out.]
Absolutely Not!”

Roo's ears drooped. "Oh well, thanks for trying, Wombat," she said, wrapping her arms around her friend.

But as Roo tried to hop away, the pain in her feet was too great. She let out a sad little whimper and collapsed to the ground.

"She'll never make it home like this!" cried Wombat. "You have to let us stay until she recovers!"

Quokka had expected to feel **gloriously powerful** at this moment, as he prepared to banish the trespassers from **his** beach.

But what he actually felt, was a far more **disappointing mix of feelings** known as:

## Misery Soup

Eew

**Ingredients:**
1 cup of anger
2 cups of stubbornness
1 tbs of jealousy
A pinch of empathy
2 litres of shame

**Method:**
Combine ingredients.
Allow to simmer.

Warning: Too much Misery Soup will result in tummy ache.

"Yeck!" cried Quokka, reacting to the unpleasant swirl in his belly (and the even more unpleasant sight of Roo's feet).

"Fine!" he yelled. Then, Quokka drew a line in the sand and scrawled 'Yours' on one side and 'Mine' on the other.

"But!" he added fiercely. "If you put so much as a whisker on my side of this line, Yowza will gladly remove it for you."

Wombat looked down at the line, which left him and Roo barely enough room to move.

"Okay, so, technically this is sharing ..." said Wombat. "But it's very unfair sharing!"

Quokka blew a raspberry and then laughed as he cartwheeled along his outrageously enormous stretch of beach.

Wombat and Roo.
Galah, Numbat and Yowza.
Quokka (cartwheeling like a rascal.)
Beach. (Quokka's bit.)
Beach. (Quokka's bit.)
Beach. (Still Quokka's bit.)
More beach. (Yep, Quokka's.)
Yet more beach. (Quokka's... of course.)
Sleeping dropbear.

“It’s okay, Wombat. Thanks for sharing, Quokka,” said Roo, before limping towards the ocean and dunking her feet in the cool water.

"Oh, sweet relief," she cried.
"Wombat, come and feel the water,
it's absolutely wonder ..."

Peeeeeeeeeeep!

A shrill whistle pierced the air.

"Oi! Roo! You are on Quokka's property. Your arm must be moved immediately,"

shouted Quokka through a makeshift megaphone.

"Yowza! Quit diggin' holes! Get out here and be a menace. Chop chop! Make it snappy!"

Roo tried to swim to her side of the line, but with every stroke, at least one part of her body poked over the imaginary line in the sand (and sea).

Peep! Peeeep! Peep!

Snap. Snap.

Flap. Flap.

Snappity. Snap! Snap!

Peeeeeeeeeeeep!

Eventually, Roo gave up and went to sit with Wombat, crouching on their tiny corner of the beach.

"We can't let that power-mad possum get away with this!" said Wombat. "We have to do something, Roo!"

"Would you like to know what I do when I'm in a tricky situation?" said Roo.

"Of course!" said Wombat.

# "Think Happy Thoughts!"

said Roo, with
a smile.

Wombat opened his
mouth to object, but Roo had
already started talking in a
Slow Calm Voice.

"Close your
eeeeyes Wombat.
Now, make a picture in your mind
of your Great Unhappiness,"
she instructed.

"Then, imagine
it disappearing. Pooofff!
And let your thoughts travel
to a happier place."

A smile suddenly spread onto Wombat's face. His thoughts had indeed travelled to a happier place. A place he liked to call … *QuokkaGetsWhatHeDeservesville.*

# PART 6

(In which Wombat tries to get even)

Roo continued talking slowly and calmly. “On the count of three we will open our eyes and feel completely at peace with the world. One, two …

**three-eek!"** cried Roo, as she woke to see Wombat aiming a large coconut at Quokka.

"What are you doing, Wombat?"

"Thinking happy thoughts!" he exclaimed.

**"Stop!"** cried Roo.

"Why?" said Wombat crossly.
"He's been mean! And selfish!"

"And you think hurting him will suddenly make him kind and happy?" said Roo.

"No," said Wombat. "But it'll make me happy!"

"Until he does the same back to you!" said Roo. "Or worse!"

"Fine," said Wombat. "But how do we make him change then?"

"We can't," said Roo. "But, what we **can** do, is enjoy our lovely little beach! We have water, shade, sand, coconuts. Plus, we have each other. And that means we have everything we need to have fun."

Wombat stomped his feet.

"**But. It's. Not. Fair,**" he insisted.

"Sometimes things just aren't fair," said Roo simply. "And that's why we have to fight to make them fair!" said Wombat, picking up two large coconuts.

Roo sighed. "Well, the only fight I'm interested in …" she said as she inched towards the sea … "is a …

water fight!"

Roo slapped her tail on the water, showering Wombat in cool wet spray. Without thinking, Wombat bomb-dived into the sea to get Roo back.

Before he knew it, Wombat was deeper than he'd ever been before.

"Hey! I can SWIM! I can SWIM!" he cried. "Wheee!"

As the water cooled Wombat's temper, he realised Roo was right. This was much more enjoyable than fighting with Quokka.

"What else can we do on a beach?" he cried.

Roo thought for a moment.

"Well, do you wanna build a sandcastle?"

"I do!" said Wombat. "Wait ... what's a sandcastle?"

Wombat soon discovered that even though their share of the beach wasn't big, it was big enough to have quite an enormous amount of fun.

"Sand is
so soft!"
"Oi!"
"Look, a
Roonicorn!"
"Eew, sea
cucumber!"
"Eew,
marsupial!"

"I'm beautiful!"

# PART 7

(In which Quokka can't get no respect)

Meanwhile, on the other side of the line, Quokka stood on his **enormous** stretch of beach, feeling like he had made an **enormous** mistake. As he glared at Wombat and Roo's joy-filled faces, he felt his own face burn with anger.

He also felt his feet burn with
Actual Hotness as the last
spot of shade disappeared from under him.

"Hot! Hot! Hot!" he cried.
"Ai! Ai! Ai!" he yelped.
"Yowzaaaaaaa!" he wailed.

"You called, Sir?" said Yowza, as he danced across the burning-hot sand.

"Not you!" shouted Quokka. "My feet! They're burning! Where did all my shade go?"

"Over there, Sir," said Yowza, pointing at Wombat and Roo. "It would appear you gave them a smaller but better portion of the beach."

"Gah!" cried Quokka.

He stormed over to the line, and tried to think of something clever to say. He settled with:

"Oi! Gimme MY beach back!"

Wombat, who was feeling the most relaxed he had ever felt in his life, raised a far more peaceful coconut at Quokka.

"Chill out!" he drawled.

"There's no neeeeed for greeeed!"

"I'm not being greedy!" boomed Quokka. "I'm being ... powerful!"

"What's so good about being powerful?" asked Roo. "I think being kind is … "

"Kind!" scoffed Quokka. "You know what **kind** animals get? They get **eaten!** But powerful animals, well, they get **respect!**"

"Respect?" said Wombat. "Never heard of it."

Quokka sighed. "It's when you get what you want because everyone's too **afraid** to say no! That's **respect!**" he said, confidently.

"I don't think that's Respect, Quokka," said Roo. "I think that's … **fear**."

"**Same thing!**" barked Quokka.

"No, it's not," said Roo. "Today, Wombat treated me in a way that made me feel cared for and important. And that makes me want to treat him the same way. I act like Wombat is *important* because he *is* important. And he treats me in the same way. That's **respect**. We wouldn't be friends without it."

"I have friends!" shouted Quokka, pointing to his crew. "More friends than you!"

Yowza scurried over to Quokka and tapped him on the foot. "We're **not** friends, Sir," he said, before scuttling away again.

"Not friends! Not friends!" screeched Galah.

"What?!" boomed Quokka.

"Well, for starters, you yell at us," said Yowza. "And you insist we call you *sir*."

"Plus, you pay us to keep you safe," added Numbat. "We're your bodyguards, not friends."

Quokka looked confused for a second. "Wait … I'm not paying you!" he yelled.

"Oh," said Numbat. Then he sighed deeply. "Right, Galah, Yowza, it's time to find ourselves a new boss."

And with that, Quokka was left on his own.

He turned to face Wombat and Roo, but suddenly felt very small. And when he felt very small there was only one thing that made him feel bigger.

A really, really, really enormous tantrum.

"This is my beach!
Mine! Mine!

Mine!

Mine!

Mine!

Mine! Mine! Mine!
All miiiiiiii..."

# PART 8

(In which Quokka reveals his true identity)

Wombat and Roo watched as a wave knocked Quokka off his feet and swept him out to sea.

"Help!" he shrieked.

"I can't swim!"

Without hesitation, Wombat and Roo worked together to rescue Quokka.

As he lay spluttering on the sand, Quokka looked up at his saviours with eyes full of sorrow and gratitude.

"Thank you," he squeaked in a very sweet, very high-pitched voice.

"Woah! What's happened to your voice?" asked Wombat.

"Oh, yes, about that...

I suppose it's time you knew the truth about me," squeaked Quokka.

And then, right before their eyes, his whole face transformed ...

into an expression so off-the-charts cute it almost made Roo's head explode with delight.

"Awwwwww!" cooed Wombat and Roo. "Too cute!"

"Hang on," said Wombat, suddenly snapping out of his stupor. "If the real you is so cute ... why were you so mean to us?"

"Because ... cuteness is a curse!" yelled Quokka, his face contorting back into a frown.

"No-one takes you seriously when you are this cute. In the wild, cuteness equals weakness. Or worse, deliciousness."

"I wanted to know what it felt like to be the big cheese, the main marsupial, the boss of the beach. So I taught myself to look and sound as menacing as I could ...

"It felt wonderful ... at first," added Quokka. "But today you showed me that in my quest for power I only made everyone else feel as small and scared as I once did. I realise now that I lost something very important along the way."

"Your sense of humour," guessed Wombat.
"Friends," said Quokka, sadly.

Wombat turned away to hide his tears.

"Are you okay?" asked Quokka.

"Yep. Good. I'm just sad that our sandcastle was washed away, that's all!" said Wombat.

"Oh look ... the line in the sand has gone too!"
cheered Roo.

Quokka stepped forward, offering Wombat and Roo his stick with a solemn bow.

"You draw it this time,"

he squeaked. "Also, I'm sorry."

Wombat picked up the stick and scratched a line into the sand. Then another. And another.

"Can I ask you a question?" squeaked Quokka.

"Sure," said Roo.

"Why did you save me?"

"It was just The Right Thing to Do," said Roo, gently.

"Oh," sighed Quokka. "So, we're not friends?"

"No," said Roo.

"Oh," said Quokka, sadly.

"But that's okay," said Roo. "Friendship takes time. Wombat and I had to climb a mountain to find out we liked each other."

“Are there any mountains around here?” asked Quokka, hopefully.

“No,” said Roo. “We do have an ocean, though.”

“But I can’t swim,” said Quokka sadly.

“Well,” said Wombat. “We’ll help you.”

And with that, Quokka, Roo and Wombat tiptoed into the water and started swimming. No, not swimming, they were splishing, sploshing and splashing. They waded through the waves, soaked in the shallows and frolicked in the foam. They laughed giddily as they let the cool water trickle over them.

As the sun sank into the sea, Quokka realised that, lifted up by the kindness and respect of his friends-to-be, he had everything he never knew he needed …

and more.

7
8
6
Numbat Knob.
5
Mt. Galah.
The Great Bullshark Bight.
4
3
Quokka's ~~The~~ Beach.
Seal Rocks.
Mt. Osprey.
Lake Lungfish.
Egret Everglades.
Regret Ridge.

# Gumshine Coast.

Scale 1 : 13,251 (or thereabouts).

Book 1

Book 2

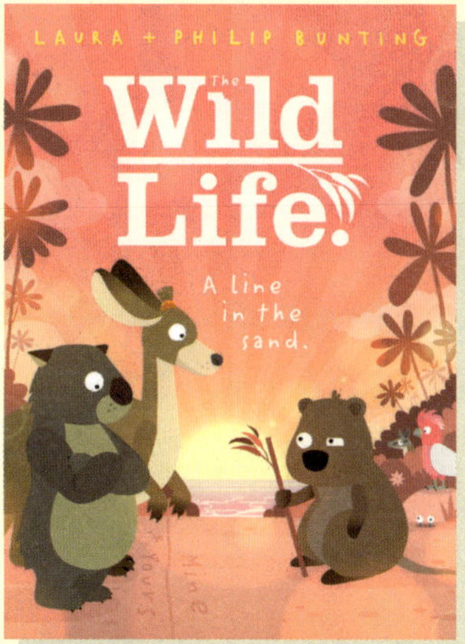

Book 3
(coming soon!)